T0147147

Order of Rule

Thomas Orion

authorHOUSE®

AuthorHouse™
1663 Liberty Drive
Bloomington, IN 47403
www.authorhouse.com
Phone: 833-262-8899

Published by AuthorHouse 09/08/2022

ISBN: 978-1-6655-7051-0 (sc)
ISBN: 978-1-6655-7050-3 (e)

Library of Congress Control Number: 2022916780

Print information available on the last page.

So it was, One Day, that the General, of the
Forces, Comanded His Order to Fight.

We are Novel, and Saint, but the Order Subsists.
There is an Strange Air About the Cores. We Sign.

So, in Order, this Air, which was a Comely Station,
Had Nothing to Do with the Regency, and So,
The Order, was a Substation to the Realm, and we,
we Decided to Order the Station.

Comando Rules.

It was Not a Nice thing, to Bring to the Soldier
in Charge, the Emperor, and we Signed this Rule
with a Sour Tint, Because the Realm was in Demise.

These Days, and I Remember, the Station was Sought,
and an Offence, in the Novel of Things, was Not
a Station, that was Desired.

We are a Combat Order.

And So we Ventured, Sign the Realm.

The Emperor Complied, and the Signature was Signed.
But in Order, the Realm, was Still His, and to
My Knowledge, He Cried a Little Bit Over the Air
of Offence at the Notion of Rule.

It Did Well.

The Officess, it Betrayed were in an Abnordance
of things and Unfinished Items.

This Said, the Order was Colose to a Halt, and
the Sign, a Regent in Dispose, was Nominal.

We Order.

No Sign is Ever Alone and the Resency, as it was
Called, Betrayed, again, an Officess, which was
Remarkable for its Conduit.

Not even Securities, were Signed.

This is One Of the Offices, which is Signed
Immediably, of Offence, that there is an Abnomen
of context wherein to Council.

We Were Order, Ordeal.

So we Began Again.

Regent, Intelligence, Order and Sign.
The Regent Himself, was Not a Bad Person, and the
Sign He Had as an Endavour, Not an Easy One, but
the Thesis, that You Order, was Not Sign.

He Felt Himself Belitteled, and In Order, a
Damage, in Sign.

These Stations, that we Endavour, is Not a Set
Frame. The Damage Concerned, is a Novel, but
the Sign is the Same, a Civilisation.

You Destroy, but More Importantly, You Build
Up. The Society that You Order, is Understood,
and While the Station is the Same, the Order
is Not.

We are Good.

The Notion of Which, the Danger of a Station,
we Settle the Score.

We are Comando.

This is it, the Station of Ores. The Entire
Universe, to Us.

We Do Not Know, but we Do, but in Order, there
Could be an Extra Dimension, there are Plenty.

But in Order, the Theory Containing One Dimension
Signs them All, so we are a Multiverse.

The Multiverse Spans, three Dimensions, Standard.
The Etherial, the Astral and the Mental Realm.

And the Concert, is are and Were, Blue Air.

What is Blue Air, Exactly. Well it is the First,
Substance. Matter has to Come from Somewhere,
so the Point is, a Philosophy.

It Existed.

Likewide did the Universe, we Sign it a Manifold,
and an Ursus at that.

But we Did Not See the Beginning.

Because this Material is in Rotation.

It Takes a Decade for it To Rotate, and that is in Order, Million Standard Years.

What is a Standard Year, well the Circle of Light on a Station, One Lightyear Out, must Commemorate the Station, and we Calculated 365 Days.

In Order of this, the Universe Looks like a Large Galaxy, and in Order it is Leveled.

North an South, is Determined by the Rotation os a Compound in Space.

The Order is Magnetism.

So we are, Standard.

The Economy is Closed, Regardless of another Dimension, Since we Signed that.

In Order, we are an Organisation, and the Sign, well the Sign is a Credit.

We Rotate, one Credit.

There is One and Only One Output. This is the
Sign, or in Order, the Revenue, that has to
be Reinvested, so in Order, Give it to the
People.

This Sounds Insane, but the Number is Signed.

Order Organisation.

This Organisation, Ours, is a Nomen. We Rule
the Entire Universe, but it Signs a Galaxy
and we Never Know, what Stable is Sign.

We Sign this, a Council.

And Here the Prince Regent, again, because
a Council, he Can Handle.

We are Order, and a Sign, and I am the
Worldwide Staff Seargeant, can be Subjected.

We want to Live, and to Survive, in Order.

What is a Cashbox, in the Lower Section 44C
on Operator, if You Mind, this is My World.

What is the Story then. Well a Hich Tech
Race, made a Mess of itself.

The Hyperspace Capacity, is Really a Space
Commemorated, by the Sages of Eld. They
Called the Astral Space.

And we Kept the Noun.

So when You Sign Astral Space, You Move.
This Order, the Subspace, went to Capacity,
When the Stardrive, was invented, this
Cycle, a Million Years Ago.

What is a Cycle, well the Time it Takes
the Galaxy to Rotate, Once.

How do You Measure this, well Electricity,
on an Order of Magnetism. The Order, How
Many we are Gravity.

But the Order was this, and this is it.
They Lived in the Astral Sphere, this
is Called Subspace Three, and they were
Angry.

It is About Right an Wrong, and Sometimes
the Order is Signed.

The Were Expanding, and in Order to Do
So, they had Breaced the Horizon, with
a Drive.

It was a Standard Drive, Level Fifteen,
which is Not Standard. We Sign Standard
Station Ten.

So this was an Enemy, with Capacity.

These Days, the Wonder of a Race, which is
in the Endavour of a Salvage, is Reprimand.

There is No Order.

The Elder Races are Minding their Own
Businesses, and the is Little Guidance.

However, there is Something.

The Nurture.

We are Many that Abode the Races of Old,
but the Sustitution of Officess, are
Nonetheless and Ordeal.

We are Officess, and we, we are in Peace.
But Not this Race, and so Order, Light.

The Race was Crystalline.

They Were an Assortment of Crystal Entities,
and the Abode was, a Nurture.

They Could Have Destroyed, the Sector they
Originated.

We assorted a Sumption, that Power was
Power and So.

So in Order, the Semblance of a Drive, on
Our Part.

The Fighting was Rife.

An Interstellar Wormhole, and a Sector,
turned Upside Down.

This was War, at the Operational Level.

Fighters, filled the Space, of the
Construct that was in an Enigmatic Pose
to the Rampage that was the Site.

I am Staff Seargeant, and as Such, I Have
to Support the Station, with the Mothership,
so that the Order of Combat is Sustain.

These Stations, that we Order, with a
Kernel, is the Administration of a Nexus,
is Not in the Order, of Status.

We Sign Blue, Green and Red.

Sign White.

But in Order of this, we Saged a Notion from
the Starbourne, the High Races.

They had Never Seen Anything Like this.

The Enemy Came from the Astral Realm, and as
Such, an Easy Prey.

But the Combination of Soft Crystal, and an
Order of Vengeance, made the Beat a Hard One.

We Had Losses, and the Damage Signed way into
the Structure.

We had a Carnage.

The Wormhole itself, which was Technology, in
Strucure, signed a Sector.

Everything was Upside Down.

But Our Capacity was Much Larger than that,
only, if they Could Get Foothold, they might
Sign a Sector, and Procede.

The Instance was Order.

We signed three Sectors Away, and Held the
Area, against the Force of the Tech Race.

We Wondered, are they Computers, in as Much
that the Construction, was one of Light and
Quartz.

Sign this, that there is a Novel.

It was an Introtech Race, and the Notion
was that of a Sun.

We Have Gods, and an Order of Nature, to
Each Planet, Endows the Nurture, Called
Core, as a Common Universal God.

This Instance, they Live in Mental Space.

Nothing Comes there.

You can Move, but in Order, if the
Consciousness is Not Tier Three, you Can
not Rest, and so with the Vessel.

The Order of God, is Such, that an Abstain
from the Order, is Such of an Order of Vile.

We Have Evil Gods. Maybe Evil Itself is the
Office, and Burtch Himself Holds that Office,
Now, But in Order, Sign Nature, and Love.

We are Officess, and I Ramble, but the Race
was Build on the Same Construction, that
Consciousness is Held By, all over the
Cosmos.

A Neural Net.

In this Case, it was a Crystal with Light
in it.

We Sign Sage.

A Novel Imbue on the Thesis that a Network
Can Carry Intelligence, is the Order of Weights

We Nominate 123, which is the Human Brain.

We are Humans, but the Alien is the Sylvian
of Eld, and the Nomen, a Werewolf.

These can Shapechange, we Call that Morphosis, and the Order of which it Takes Place, is an order of Two, Three Seconds.

We Sign these, the Order of Our Universe.

Well, we Won the War, and the Wormhole, in Space, Our Space, was Closed, and a Pin, a Sentry, was Set up to Monitor, any Future Activity, in that Sector.

This is it, we Sign.

The Regent wa Unhappy with His Lot, so we Decided to Run Him through the Machine.

In Order of that, the Stabs Division.

Nothing is Harder than the Stab, and a Sovereign Notion is that of a Cores.

We are not "Hardcore", but we Sign Hard, Cores, and that.

He Did well, which was Expected. They are
Tough, the Breed, but He Wanted to Further
the Course a Bit, So we Added Art.

Art is the Nomen. It is the Movement of
Astral Energy, and Can give Rise to
Illusions, and Actual Manifestation.

A Manifestation, is Not Nice.

There are Worms.

These Worms are Illusions, and the Fear
of them, can Fuel a Manifestation with
Energy.

Only the Control of Fear, will Keep the
Menace from Manifestation.

There are Orders, the Livelyhood of
Flowers and the Joy of Little Children,
which is in the Envue of the Priestess.

Considering that, the Regent Fell for a
small Division of the Cores.

A Loner, and a Combatant in Her Own, and we do Sign Women, I Mean, they Order well in Hand to Hand, and the Rest Can Not be Denied.

In Order of this, a Fighter.

They Wanted to Wait with the Marriage, and the Lord Himself Designed a Notion that would Last.

The Empress Esquire.

She Was Called Bunjip, and a Sovereign Brunette, Tending on the Dark.

The Red Spot was there.

Her Humour.

So all went well, and they Consumed the Marriage, but in Order, this is it, She Inorgurated His Officess as Leader, Because, O no, I Forget One thing.

Administration, which was the First,
and Extended Course, that He Recieved.

He Signed the Ledger Well.
Credit, Organisation, Order.

The Order was this.
We are at Arms.

So the Day Came, when the Lord would
Resume His Officess and Order, a Universe,
Now Turned Around, and On Rails.

We Signed, this.

The Order, Itself was a Masterpiece, the
Order was a Credit, in Revolution.

This is it.

When there is Just One Economy, as Said,
it Must be in Revolution.

The Order Stands.

And we Sign.

One Of these Days, I am Going to Get
Myself a Memory.

Because I Forgot this.

The Empress, Now Princess, was in a Mood
of Orderly, and She Signed the Class
Concerning Art.

A Teatrical, Because She was Under the
Diety, Love.

And as Such, She Got Powers.
Kinetics, Armour and Healing.

She was Devastation.

The Armour was an Electron Harness, and
the Sign Silver.

The Armour, and Comfortably So, of the
Emperor, Now Imperoar in Love, was that
of an Iron Harness, and Red.

In Order of this, and I Sign Again. The
Station of the Couple, was One of Respect
and Honour.

We Signed, Stable.

These Notions, that we are a Commonwealth,
and that we Engender the Nurture of the State,
is a Condemoniom of a Sage.

The Gods were there.

They are Walking the Earth, and this is it,
the Notion of these, are the Daunt.

We Saviour the Tract, of Magic and Power.

The Power Scale on Art, was Remarkably in
Reach for the Liege.

And Eternity.

He Was Undying, and So was the Princess. They
ordered a Lucrative, and Esquire, with Several
Orders of the Nurture, a Station of a Thousand
Years.

Commonwealth, is This.

These Omens are for Sale.

We Commit Nothing with the Atrocity of the Offends
that Cause a Scare.

We Wanted to Sign the Crystal Effect Shut.

That Meant that we Needed to Go in there, and
there Meant the Astral Realm, and that Meant
More Art.

Art was Not His Strong Side, although Powers,
but He Wanted to Join the Operation, and Silver,
as His Princess was Called, wanted to Come Along.

There are So Many things You can Do, as a Reign,
but Stab Operations, are One of them, so Order.

The Princess, whom had invented Har Own Name,
was Called Lunai Univesus.

And Her Power, Liquid Silver.

Here Comes the Order.

Liquid Silver was Pivotal for the Operation.
The Alien Powers, Came from a Source, that
Resonated in the Same Spectrum.

And the Core, His Majesty Himself.

Now a Provess, having Trained, and as a Nomen
a Frame to be Reconed With.

We Sign these Orders.

These Days, the Nomen Of an Operation, is
the Central Core, that is Pivotal.

And in this Case, Something with Iron. Since
their Power was Red.

Also, the Administration, as a Being You Have
to Have One, was in Intelligence.

We Came Up with Aught.

So again, we Ventured, go There.

This was Disastrous, the Core was Shut, but
the Mechanism, Controlling it, as Operational.

These Signs, of Something, that Endavour an
Act of Art, are Such that You Fear.

This Fear is Subdued.

So is Also, with the Emotion Controlling is.
It is Important to Stay Cognitive.

The Prince was a Master, and His Spouse, even
More So.

They Went in, through a Double Energy Vortex,
and the Remains, a Captain with a Stomach.

These Signs, that we are, the Best, is in
Vanguard of the Novel, that we Pursue.

Also, the Notion of an Honour, that we are,
Soldiers, and that we Sign Order.

There is Nothing in this World, which is Not
in Danger of Destruction, and we Sign the
Solution to Peace, an Order.

The Station as Such, was in Terror, and that
Little Fear, Came Upon Us, with this.

Worms.

The Captain Said, that a Radio Signal, had
Reached the Outer Limit.

The Signal, Caused some Fear.

"I am in Trance."
"The Fear is Subdued."
"We have Worms."

This Order, that Some of the Corporal was
Down, Troubled the Seargeant Immensely.

"We are at Nurture, Send the Corporal In."

This Session, that the Stab, was Not Enough,
Had its Toil, among the Corporals.

"This Session, will End."
"I Wonder, about this."

The Wonder was Of Course, Art.

The Signal was Given, and the Seargeant,
thought, it Would be Wise, to Engender,
the Stabe with a Corporal.

They Went in.

Inside, the World was a Vortex of Energy,
that Took Form, and Cased itself in Boxes
and Pyramids, alike.

One of these Boxes, Housed the Stab.

Inside, the World was a Maze of Tunnels and
Corridors, Leading into Smaller Boxes, with
Energy in them.

The Stab was Around, but So was the Enemy.
We Found that the Status was Fully Fucked
Up, and that the Princess was Missing.

She was the Best Telepath, and we are in
Wonder about the Stance.

Afterwards, she Told Us that She had had
an Inside Out Phenomena, which was Undescribed,
as of the Codex of the Art.

It is Called that, Because of the Emotional
Issue, Stay Calm.

So We Went in, and Stated to Look for the Enemy.
They Had to Be Around Somewhere, and the Order,
the Unit of the Stab, Also.

The Stab was Alive, but in Deep Art.

The Art Section, is Such, You can Cancel it
with Technology, Just Throw a Sparque.

We Installed the Module, and with a Little
bit of Ease, the Station Cleared.

They were in Glow Worms, and Flashes.

Now the Station was this, We had to Find the
Center, and Document the Aliens.

This was an Anteroom, and the Real Hasle,
Was Straight Ahead.

Into the Cube.

The Cube was a Maze, Again, and we Signed an
Order of Aliens, that were, Crystal.

They Lived Here.

This Notion, that the Hemisphere, was an Order,
of Sign, was New to the Art.

They were Electric.

So, ontowards, we Levied the Art with Technology,
and we Signed, the Station.

They were Astral Entities, and they Had Accidentally
Blown a Hole, in their Subspace.

We Helped them Get Along.

This was It.

This is Noun and I Say, these Instances are my Lovel.
There are No Sciences, that Occur without a Sign.

These Instances are Mine.

There are Three things that you Need to Remember
when You are Dealing with Eternity.

No One Lives forever, not Even a Stellar Liege,
but for the Reference, a Thousand Years is a Long
time.

His Espouse, the Princess Wanted a Real Estated
Wedding, with Silver and White, Dress, and the
Spouse, in Order of that.

She was Estemed, to Live for another Eight Hundred
Years, and the Wedding was Supposed to Reflect
that.

We are in Wonder.

So the Wedding Occured, and the White Sash of the
Princess, was Decorated with Gold, so as to
Emphasize the Nurture of the Lord.

We are a Statement of the Officess, and the Order, well we Went On to Secure the Univers, as Large as it Is.

These Strange Emotions, that we Sign, we Order and we Copy, these are, that the Notion is Sound.

Pletipas and Ingenuire is Not the Notion if You Want to Sign Eternity, and the Novel of it, well that is the Strange Emotion that you Get, when You Do Something Right.

The Notion of this.
Order.

Printed in the United States
by Baker & Taylor Publisher Services